£6.99

GW00373900

LOONEY TUNES ™

This book belongs to:

Name...

Age ....

Date ....

My favourite Looney Tunes characters are ....

....

....

WALL OF FAME!

WASSUP!

No kiddin'! Your very own Looney Tunes annual eh Doc? Better get toinin' the pages for some sheer lunacy!

FISHY BUSINESS!

HELP BUGS FIND A CLEAR ROUTE THROUGH THE MAZE SO HE CAN NAB THE CATCH OF THE DAY!

START!

FINISH!

7

FIND THAT TOON!

Can you find the names of some of our Looney Tunes in our word search? They can be read up, down, horizontally and vertically!

Tweety   Sylvester

Bugs Bunny   Daffy Duck   Wile E. Coyote

Granny   Speedy Gonzales   Tasmanian Devil   Porky Pig

Marc Anthony   Pussyfoot   Petunia Pig

Road Runner   She Devil   Hector

Yosemite Sam   Elmer Fudd   Lola Bunny   Penelope Le Pew

K	S	E	L	A	Z	N	O	G	Y	D	E	E	P	S
B	O	O	T	P	K	T	L	P	S	O	L	S	T	O
O	U	H	Y	O	S	E	M	I	T	E	S	A	M	S
S	T	G	P	E	T	O	Y	O	C	E	E	L	I	W
H	P	T	S	K	S	D	H	D	T	S	P	T	T	R
S	P	H	H	B	D	S	P	D	K	P	L	A	H	O
P	L	T	E	O	U	T	O	A	D	L	P	S	K	A
E	T	S	D	D	Y	N	P	F	D	S	L	M	T	D
T	U	Y	E	W	N	K	N	F	F	D	K	O	S	R
U	N	L	V	E	O	T	P	Y	U	L	L	A	R	U
N	I	S	V	I	P	H	O	P	D	F	H	N	L	N
I	A	L	I	L	E	T	S	G	U	R	S	B	A	N
A	P	O	T	S	E	N	O	S	C	E	O	U	D	E
P	I	G	T	S	E	A	L	D	K	M	T	N	N	R
I	G	F	S	E	P	P	C	P	A	G	L	P	E	S
G	L	Y	S	O	R	S	T	W	E	E	T	Y	L	T
L	T	S	O	T	L	A	S	G	O	H	G	N	I	O
T	S	S	O	L	E	M	P	T	D	G	L	N	L	L
S	L	U	H	T	P	N	T	O	P	P	A	K	P	K
P	P	L	S	P	O	R	K	Y	P	I	G	K	G	P

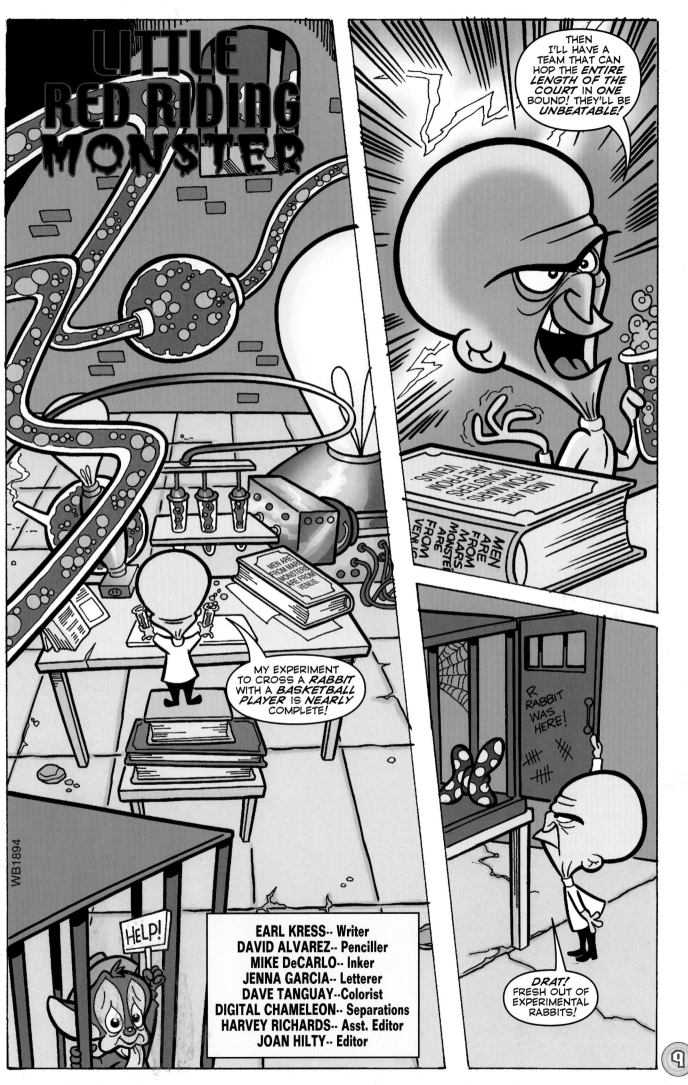

LITTLE RED RIDING MONSTER

THEN I'LL HAVE A TEAM THAT CAN HOP THE *ENTIRE LENGTH OF THE COURT* IN ONE BOUND! THEY'LL BE *UNBEATABLE!*

MEN ARE FROM MARS, MONSTERS ARE FROM VENUS.

MY EXPERIMENT TO CROSS A *RABBIT* WITH A *BASKETBALL PLAYER* IS *NEARLY* COMPLETE!

R RABBIT WAS HERE!

DRAT! FRESH OUT OF EXPERIMENTAL RABBITS!

HELP!

WB1894

EARL KRESS -- Writer
DAVID ALVAREZ -- Penciller
MIKE DeCARLO -- Inker
JENNA GARCIA -- Letterer
DAVE TANGUAY -- Colorist
DIGITAL CHAMELEON -- Separations
HARVEY RICHARDS -- Asst. Editor
JOAN HILTY -- Editor

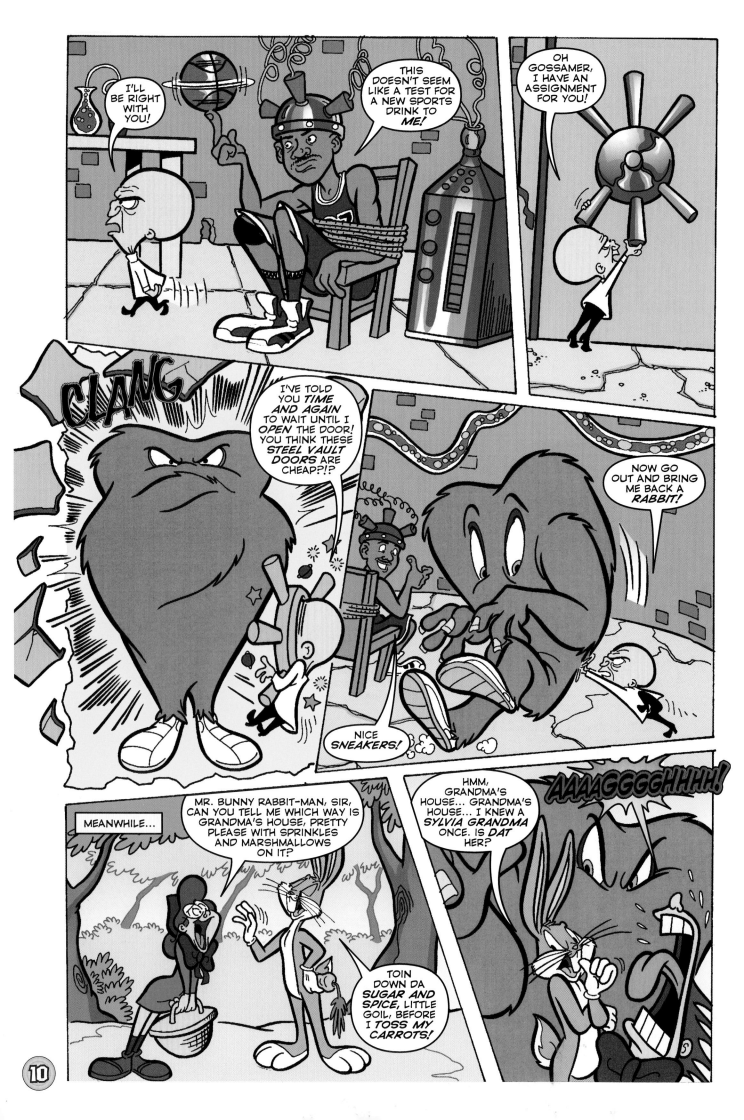

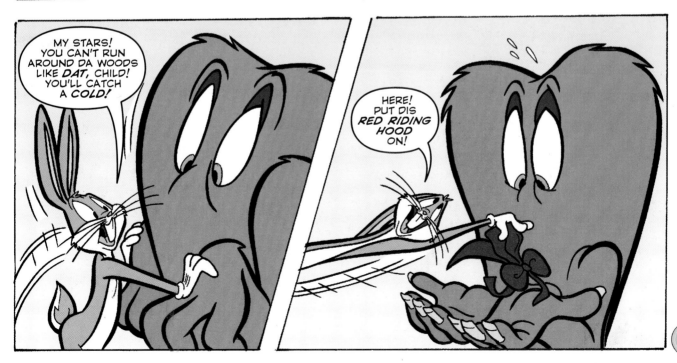

YA FOLLOW DA *DIRT ROAD* UNTIL YOU COME TO DA *FORK* IN DA ROAD. PICK UP DA FORK AND YOU CAN'T MISS GRANNY'S HOUSE!

THANKS, BUDDY! I WON'T FORGET YOU FOR THIS!

I'LL MAKE SO*ITAIN* HE DON'T FORGET!

NOW TO BEAT DOSE TWO GOONS TO GRANNY'S!

...AND THE MONSTER WAS *RED* AND *HAIRY! ALMOST* AS HAIRY AS *GRANDPA!*

LAND SAKES, CHILD! NOW, WHO COULD *THAT* BE AT THE DOOR?

PA'DON ME, SIR! IS DA *LADY* OF DA HOUSE HOME?

I'M THE LADY OF THE HOUSE!

GOOD ONE, CHUM!

BUT OKAY, I'LL PLAY ALONG. *I* CAN TAKE A JOKE AS WELL AS DA *NEXT* FELLA!

HERE, TAKE RED TO DA MOVIES. BUT DON'T SEE A *HORROR FLICK*. DEY MIGHT T'INK YOU *ESCAPED* FROM DA PICTURE!

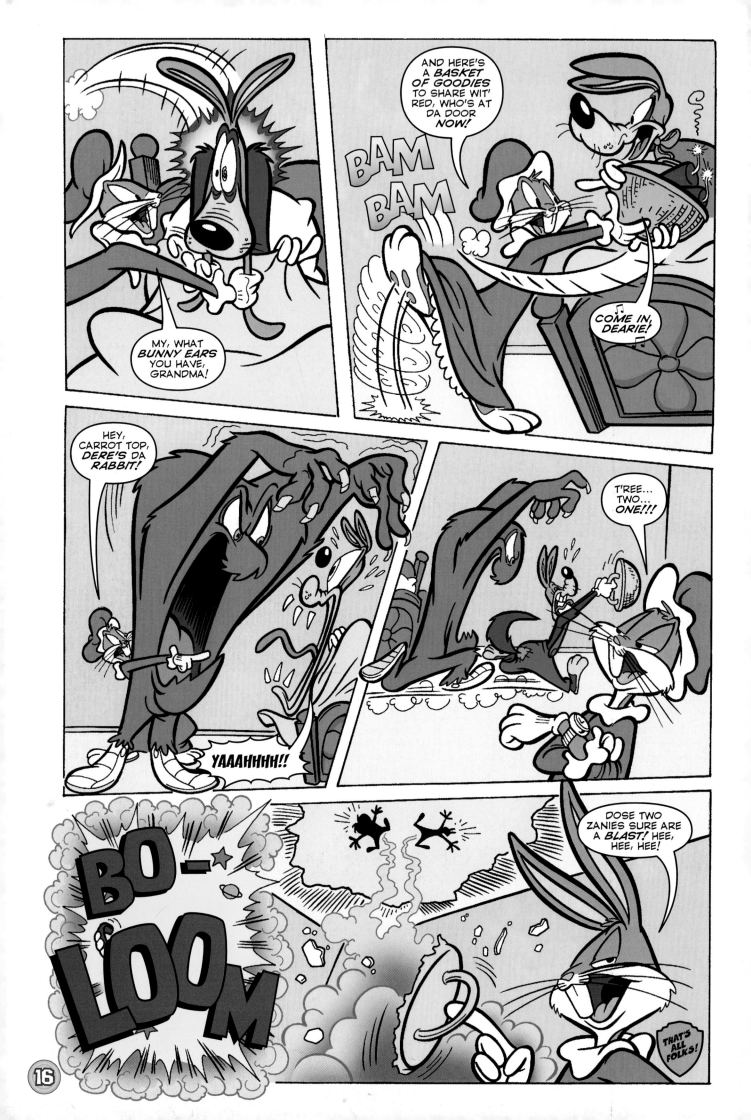

DASHING DAFFY!

Looks like Porky Pig's got Daffy on the Run! Of all the smaller images of Daffy running scared, only one is the same as the main picture. Can you Spot it?

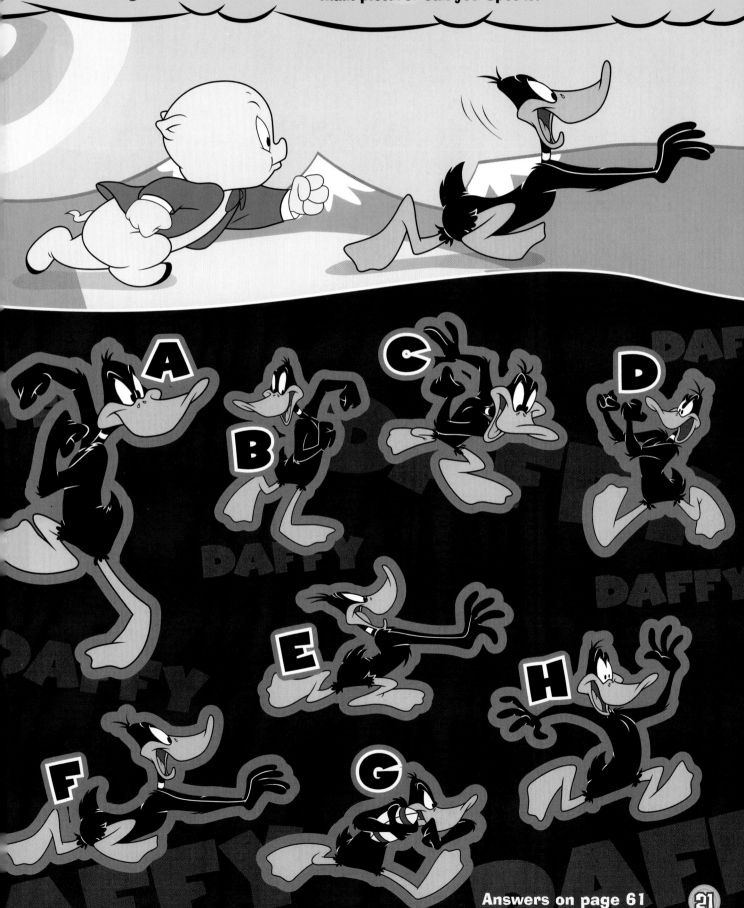

Answers on page 61

A FULL HEAD O'HARE

Writer: Terry Collins
Penciller: Pablo Zamboni
Inker: Ruben Torreiro
Letterer: Daniel Griffo
Colorist: Prismacolor

OH, *THAT.* HEH-HEH-HEH. I GET A WITTLE MIXED UP SOMETIMES. *PWONOUN TWOUBLE.*

UM, RIGHT. WHY DON'T YOU SIT DOWN AND LET'S TALK ABOUT IT, HMMM?

ACCORDING TO YOUR FILE, YOU'RE A VERY *NICE* MAN. KIND TO CHILDREN,,, HELPFUL TO OLD LADIES,,, CHAIRMAN OF YOUR COMMUNITY WATCH PROGRAM,,,

AND DON'T FOWGET I'M TOP IN MY DISTWICT FOR *AWUMINUM SIDING SALES!*

YET ON WEEKENDS YOU ENJOY WEARING CAMOUFLAGE CLOTHING AND STALKING DEFENSELESS, WOODLAND CREATURES!

EVEWYBODY NEEDS A *HOBBY!*

I AGREE, BUT YOUR HOBBY DOESN'T MATCH YOUR *PSYCHE* PROFILE. TEL ME,,, WHAT IS YOUR *SUCCESS* RATE?

OH, I'M AN EXCEWWENT SALESMAN--WOULD YOU LIKE TO SEE OUR SPECIAL THIS MONTH? FWEE VINYL SHUTTERS INCWUDED IN THE PWICE!

NO, NO--I WAS TALKING ABOUT YOUR SUCCESS IN CATCHING WILD GAME. HOW'S YOUR *TWOPHY*--ER, *TROPHY* WALL LOOKING.

WELL,,, NOT VEWY GOOD, I'M AFWAID. I NEVER SEEM TO BWING ANYTHING HOME BUT SORE FEET.

23

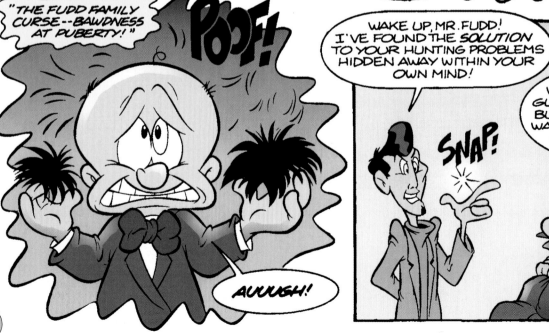

NO, NOTHING SO *DRASTIC!* MY FRIEND, *YOU*, ARE A FRUSTRATED FELLOW! YOU HUNT RABBITS ,,,"*HARES*",,, IN A SUBCONSCIOUS QUEST TO RECLAIM YOUR OWN LOST "*HAIR*"!

I AM? I DO?

I'VE CHECKED YOUR MEDICAL CHARTS. THERE'S NO *SCIENTIFIC* REASON WHY YOU ARE BALD! IT'S ALL IN YOUR *HEAD*...SO TO SPEAK

I PREDICT IF YOU CAN START BEING *NICE* TO RABBITS, YOUR HAIR WILL COME BACK AND END THIS *DESTRUCTIVE* CYCLE.

STOP CHASING WABBITS? I DUNNO,,, I GUESS I COULD *TWY*...

OKAY! I'LL STAWT FIWST THING *TOMOWWOW!* THANKS FOR EVEWYTHING, *DOCTOR NOGGIN!*

SAY, WHERE'S MY *GUN*?

OH, I'LL HOLD ONTO THAT UNTIL YOU'VE *COMPLETED* THE TREATMENT,,,

...AND AFTER YOU'VE GOTTEN MY *BILL!*

TWO WEEKS LATER...

BOY, SURE HAS BEEN *QUIET* SINCE FUDDSIE GAVE UP CHASIN' ME AROUND THE FOREST.

USUALLY, I AIN'T ONE TO *MEDDLE*, BUT I THINK HE NEEDS A LITTLE *NUDGE* BACK INTA ACTION, COITESY OF AL'S BAKERY.

DING! DONG!

YES...? WHO IS IT?

SPLAT!

OH, HEWWO, WABBIT. *PWEASE*, COME *INSIDE*--WOULD YOU WIKE A COLD GWASS OF MILK? I JUST WOVE MILK WITH PIE! OR WOULD YOU PWEFER *CAWWOT JUICE?*

CARROT JUICE? NOW YOU'RE TALKING, DOC! I'LL TAKE A SIP OR TWO, --SURE

NOW CUT DAT OUT! YOU AIN'T SUPPOSED TO BE *POLITE* AFTER I BEAN YOU WITH A PIE!

I'M NOT?

NO! YOU'RE *SCARIN'* ME WID THE "KINDER, GENTLER" *ACT!*

SPARRING PARTNERS!

It's common knowledge that some of our Looney Tunes don't always see eye-to-eye! Draw lines to match up each character with his adversary!

Answers on page 61!

WHICH WILE E.?

Can you spot which of Wile E. Coyote's shadows matches the main image of him on the left?

A

B

C

D

E

F

G

Answer on page 61!

33

Copyright ©1996 Warner Bros. All rights reserved. The Looney Tunes Characters, their distinctive likenesses, and all related characters, slogans, and indicia are the property and trademarks of Warner Bros., a Time Warner Entertainment Company. Published under license.

34

Writer: Mark McKain Penciller: Omar Aranda (Sol Studio) Inker: Scott McRae Letterer: Bob Pinaha

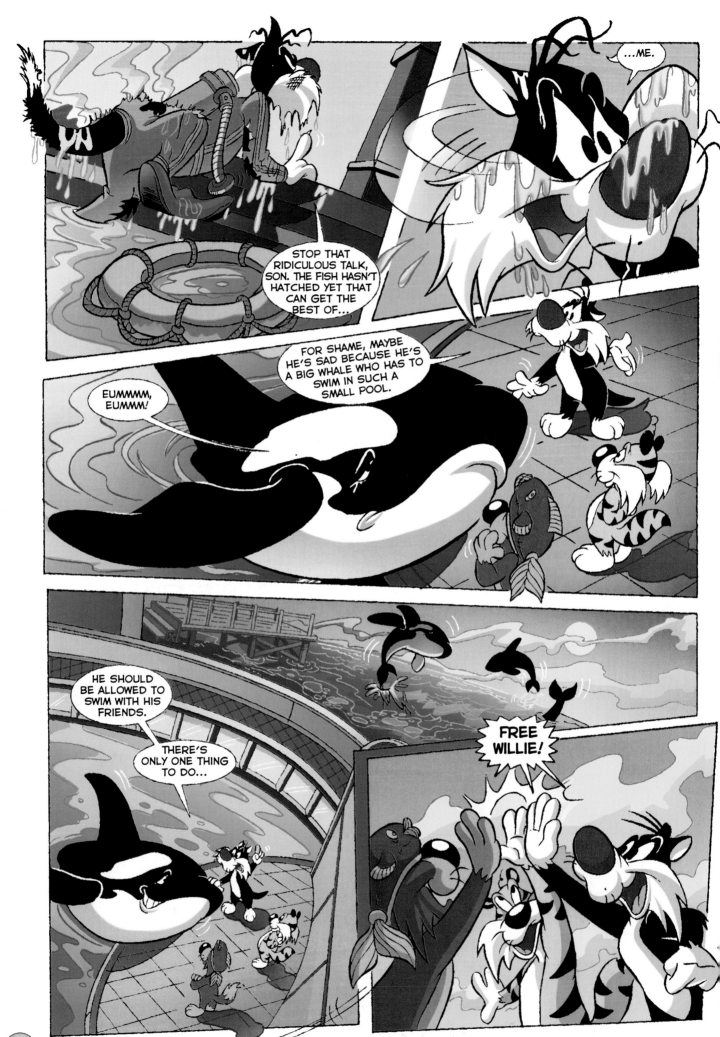

PROP-ER MATCH!

There are some things our 'toons just can't do without! Can you match up each character to his (or her) correct prop?

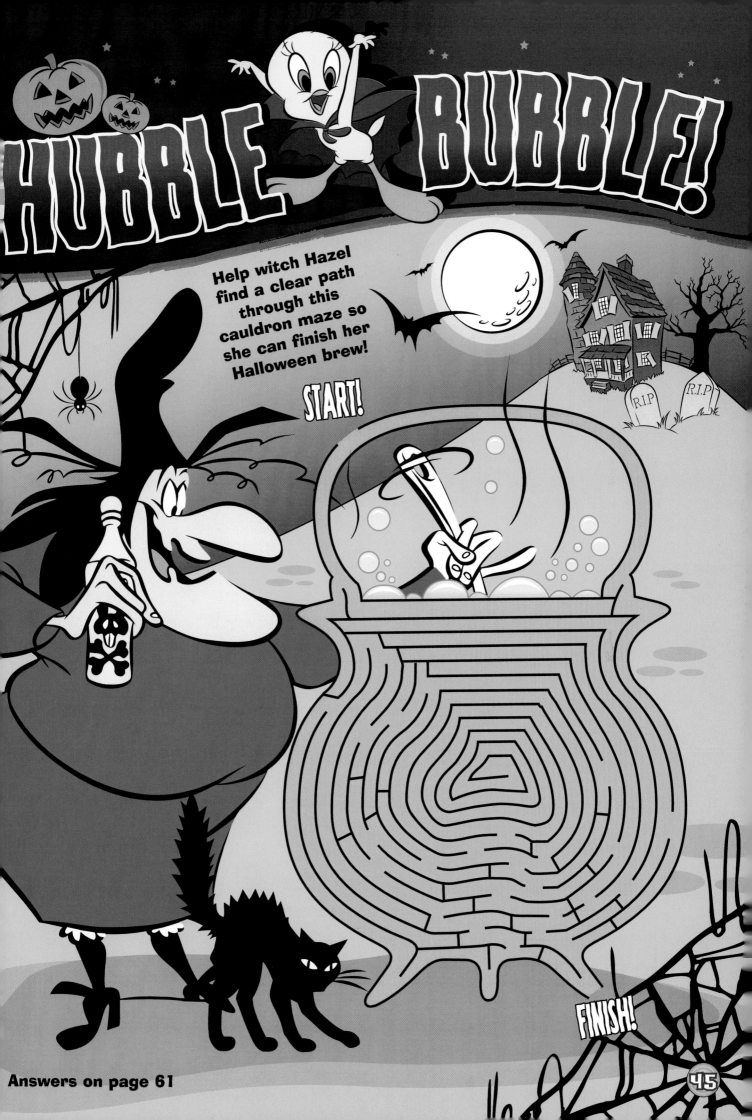

FEAST OF COLOUR!

Colour in this picture of Granny and
Tweety celebrating Thanksgiving!

Prickly Problems in Caktuspantz!

BOBBI JG WEISS—Writer
WALTER CARZON—Penciller
HORACIO OTTOLINI—Inker
JENNA GARCIA—Letterer
DAVE TANGUAY—Colorist
DIGITAL CHAMELEON—Separations
HARVEY RICHARDS—Asst. Editor
JOAN HILTY—Editor

CAKTUSPANTZ, TEXAS.

WELL, DEPUTY, THANK GOODNESS IT'S *FRIDAY!* TIME TO SPEND A NICE, QUIET *WEEKEND* IN SOME FRIENDLY OLD WESTERN *TOWN!*

WESTERN-TYPE HERO

OH, YES, THAT SOUNDS DELI–...DELU–... *LOVELY!* I'M SO THIRSTY I COULD DRINK A WHOLE *WELL* DRY!

COMEDY RELIEF

WB#1888

TEN *VANILLA MILKSHAKES,* BARTENDER, WITH A ROUND OF *DECAF CACTUS COLA* CHASERS!

I LIKE A GOOD *SUGAR RUSH* NOW AND THEN, BUT CAFFEINE'LL *KILL* YA!

DON'T *WORRY,* DEPUTY, I'LL HAVE THIS ALL SORTED OUT IN A *JIFF!*

NOW FOR A QUICK PERUSAL OF THE *WANTED POSTERS* IN THE *SHERIFF'S OFFICE!*

I'LL FIND SOME WIMPY BAD GUY TO ARREST, COLLECT THE BOUNTY AND *PAY* THE BARTENDER'S *TAB!*

THIS OUGHTTA DO IT!

CHICKEN INSPECTOR

LAWN JOCKEY

BOUNTY HUNTER

ROACH WRANGLER

BINGO! *THIS* GUY'LL BE A *BREEZE* TO CATCH!

TOO LATE. *GRANNY JONES* BROUGHT HIM IN JUST *YESTERDEE.*

THEN *THIS* ONE--

LIMPIN' LARADO CAUGHT HIM THIS *MORNING.*

WANTED MILQUETOAST MANGER REWARD $000

WANTED GOMEZ McFILIROTY REWARD $2000

WANTED FLATSCAN KID $1000

WANTED SCRUFFY McDOODLE REWARD $000

WANTED FLATSCAN KID REWARD $1000

HIM?

THE TOWN *KINDERGARTEN CLASS* CORNERED HIM AT THE PLAYGROUND AN *HOUR AGO.*

LENNY "THE NOSE" BIGGUN REWARD $500

TURNED HIMSELF IN AT THE *POUND* JUST A'FORE *YOU* SHOWED UP.

BAD LAD REWARD $1.50

IF Y'WANT *BOUNTY MONEY,* STRANGER, LOOKS LIKE YER GONNA HAVE TO CATCH *HIM!*

NASTY CANASTA ATTLE RUSTLER, HORSE THIEF, DUCK HUNTER REWARD $100,000

GOMEZ McGILIKUTY REWARD $2000

ATSCAN KID REWARD $1000

SCRUFFY McDOODLE REWARD $800

ULP.

PFFT! I'LL HAVE HIM *BEHIND BARS* BEFORE YOU CAN SAY "PETER PICKED A PIPER'S PICKLED..."

...UH, "PETER PIPER PICKLED A PICKING..."

...UH, "PIPER PETER POKED A..." UHHH...

I'LL HAVE HIM BEHIND BARS *REAL QUICK!*

CODED CHARACTERS!

WRITE DOWN THE FIRST LETTER OF EACH CHARACTER'S NAME FOR EVERY TIME IT APPEARS. UNJUMBLE THEM, AND FILL IN THE MISSING VOWELS, TO REVEAL A FAMOUS LOONEY TUNES PHRASE!

VOWELS

A
O
A

☐ ☐ ☐ ☐ ☐ ☐ ' ☐ ☐ ☐ ☐ ☐ ☐ ☐ ☐ ☐ !

Answers on page 61

57

Wile E. Coyote and Road Runner

IN DATED REFERENCE

WB 1620

Writers: S.Carolan & J.Moore Pencils: D.Alvarez Inks: M.DeCarlo Letters: J.Costanza Colors: D.Tanguay Edits: D.Kurtin

LOONEY TUNES, characters, names, and all related indicia are trademarks of Warner Bros. ©1999.

LOONEY SOLUTIONS!

BIRO
Beep
Beep

Page 6
Golfing Gaffes! ✓

Well Done

Page 7
Fishy Business!

Good effort! ✓

Page 8 ✓
Find that 'Tune!

Page 21 ✓
Dashing Daffy!
F is the same.

Pages 18-20 ✓
Please leave your message...
Phone 1- Daffy Duck, Phone 2- Bugs Bunny, Phone 3- Elmer Fudd, Phone 4- Pepé Le Pew, Phone 5 - Foghorn Leghorn, Phone 6 - Wile E. Coyote, Phone 7 - Taz, Phone 8 - Tweety Pie, Phone 9 - Yosemite Sam, Phone 10 - Sylvester, Phone 11 - Speedy Gonzales, Phone 12 - Marvin the Martian.

Well Done

Page 32 ✓
Sparring Partners!
Elmer Fudd and Bugs Bunny, Porky Pig and Daffy Duck, Sylvester and Tweety Pie, Road Runner and Wile E. Coyote, Foghorn Leghorn and Henery Hawk.

Page 33 ✓
Which Wile E?
F is the matching shadow.

Pepe 4 Penelope

Page 44 ✓ *Excellent!*
Prop-er Match!

1	2	3	4	5	6	7	8
A	F	E	D	H	B	G	C

Page 45 ✓
Hubble Bubble!

Page 17 ✓
Canine Confusion!
Trail B leads to K-9

Well Done

Page 57 ✓
Coded Characters!
That's all folks!